T-BOY OF THE BAYOU

by Wayne T. McGaw
pictures by George Crespo

Happy Reading!

Carolrhoda Books, Inc. / Minneapolis

Down in Louisiana, near the bayou, not far from the Gulf of Mexico, lived a young boy.

His daddy had red hair, and he had red hair. To their neighbors, the daddy was Grand Rouge or Big Red, and because the boy had red hair, too, he was called Petit Rouge or T-Rouge.

The young boy's real name was Gatien Alcide Campo, but he didn't mind people calling him T-Rouge or sometimes T-Boy. His

momma mostly called him T-Boy, and it made him happiest to hear it when she kissed him awake to go help his daddy with the nets.

T-Boy's daddy was a shrimper. It was hard work, but his daddy was a jolly man who never complained. The boy's family had a shrimp boat called the *Joie De Vivre*. His momma and daddy said the joy of life was everything. That's what the boat's name stood for. You enjoyed what the Gulf gave you, whether it was an empty net or a full one.

Late one night, after he had turned off the kerosene lamp by his bed, T-Boy heard his parents talking in the kitchen.

His daddy said, "Well, Momma, if I don't get some s'rimps soon, we gonna have trouble, yeah."

"They'll be here soon, baby, don't worry."

"Oh, we'll make it, but duh s'rimps just ain't dere. I made more drags dan ever, and nuttin'. Duh cleanest drag I done ever seen. Not even no jellyfish."

"Well, it'll change."

T-Boy was worried.

The next morning, T-Boy lay on the grassy edge of the bayou and wished he could help find the shrimp for his daddy. He wished so hard that the words popped right out of his mouth. And as the sound of his wish rippled across the bayou, he heard a voice say, "I can make yuh wish come true."

T-Boy looked all around but didn't see anyone, until finally he noticed a thin green snake sunning itself on the bank near the cattails. He sneaked up behind it, as quiet as he could, and whispered, "Excuse me, Mr. Green Snake, were you just talking to me? Psst, Mr. Snake. . . "

"Never hiss at a snake, boy." A voice came from within the reeds. "Yuh can whisper all day to dat ol' snake, but he's a little hard to hearin'."

"Wh . . . who. . . , " T-Boy stammered. "Who are you? Where are you?"

Out of the thicket of reeds walked a marsh heron.

"Don't look so shocked, T-Boy. Dere are worlds wit'in worlds. Don't tink because yuh ain't seen sometin', it don't exist. Now den, I can grant yuh wish, T-Boy. I can hep yuh hep yuh momma and daddy. I can show yuh where duh s'rimps are, and duh crabs, too."

"Oh, please, Mr. Heron. Please."

"I can hep, but yuh'll have to do sometin', too."

"Oh, anything, Mr. Heron. Anything."

"Not so fast," the heron told T-Boy. "Lemme s'plain. I can show yuh where duh s'rimps are, but I can't make dem come out to yuh daddy's net, no."

"Show me. Show me. I'll get 'em out."

Then the heron leaned back, bounced on his thin legs, and lifted into the air without losing a feather. He called from above the boy's head, "Don't just stand dere, boy. Follow me."

T-Boy ran to the dock, jumped into his pirogue, untied it, and paddled beneath the heron. Down the bayou he went, into the marsh, through many, many narrow canals, until the heron landed feet first beside him in the shallows and said, "Dere dey are. Trapped in dat lake. Somehow duh pass got silted up. I tink too many boats been comin' and goin', and duh shore done fallen in."

The boy could see a big clump of mud and grass blocking a small opening.

"Duh s'rimps need to get to duh deep water of duh Gulf, T-Boy. If dey don't, ain't gonna be no s'rimps next year. Wit'out s'rimps, duh fish gonna suffer. Wit'out fish, duh birds suffer. Duh whole marsh suffers, and, as yuh know, dat includes s'rimpers like yuh people. It's like duh seasons. Everyting's got its time, yeah. Everybody in dis world's connected."

"Well," said T-Boy, "I'll just move that mud and let the shrimp out. Then everybody'll be happy."

And the boy paddled to the little pass and tried to move the mud. But try as he might, he could not make headway. He used his paddle like a shovel, but every bladeful of wet mud he picked up was replaced with another "plop!" from the shore. He needed help, and it was getting dark.

"T-Boy, yuh not gonna make it by yuhsef, and I can't move much," the heron said, as he flicked a bit of sludge from his beak.

"What can I do?" the boy asked.

The heron said, "I have only one more suggestion, but I don't tink yuh gonna like it, no."

"What?"

"I can change yuh into a crab, and yuh can get all duh uddah crabs to dig a way out."

"A crab? Change me into a crab? I don't want to be no crab!"

"T-Boy. Crabs ain't all dat bad. People are always judging tings by looks. Sweetest creature I ever met was a Blue-Claw she-crab from Last Island. Shed her shell right off her back to hep. Sure would. Right off her back."

"Why would I want to be a crab?"

"Crabs will only take orders from anuddah sea creature. Dey won't listen to me. I'm not a sea creature. I'm a sky creature — well, a little land and some sea mixed in."

"Could I be something else?" T-Boy asked. "A red fish?"

"Poisson Rouge? Well, don't see why not. But when yuh change, yuh can't change back."

"What? I'd have to be a fish forever?"

"Well, yeah, but dat ain't half bad — never have to take a bath."

"I dunno, Mr. Heron."

"There's no uddah way, T-Boy. No uddah way to hep yuh parents — or duh s'rimps."

"Well . . . uh . . . if there's no other way, I'll do it."

The heron uttered three chirps, followed by a trill and a caw, while he circled T-Boy in the pirogue. He fluttered up and down, and, quick as that, T-Boy was in the water, his tail swirling in the current, his scales shimmering in the clean water. He called all the sea creatures together: the crabs (those with their own shells and those in borrowed shells) and the fish (red fish, specks, mullets, croakers, and minnows). They worked and worked. Even the crawfish helped. By the time the moon came up, the shrimp were free!

"Now," T-Boy thought. "Now to get the shrimp down to the *Joie De Vivre*." And he herded the shrimp through the marsh out into the bayou toward the Gulf. He swam from shore to shore, chasing stragglers back into the school. He swam fast with his back out of the water to speed them through the straight parts of the bayou, and he swam deep to slow them around the bends. As he neared the bridge by Isle D'Chenier, he stuck his head from the water.

He could see his father's boat, but something was wrong — the *Joie De Vivre*'s nets were up. They weren't in the water. So, he raced ahead to the boat. He saw his daddy leaning against the pick board. His momma was there, too. They were crying. "Where is my T-Boy? Where he be?"

He called up to them, "Here, I'm here."

But T-Boy's parents couldn't hear him.

Just then, Mr. Heron flew down and landed on T-Boy's daddy's shoulder.

"What duh heck?" said his daddy. And he brushed the heron off. Then the heron went to T-Boy's momma, then his daddy, then his momma. Then he landed on the side of the board and peered into the dark water.

"What's dat fool bird doin'?"

"What's he looking at?"

"Oh. Dere's sum pretty red down dere, yeah," T-Boy's daddy said.

Then T-Boy lifted his head from the water and called, "Daddy! Momma!"

"T-Boy?" they both answered. "T-Boy! Where?"

"Down here," yelled T-Boy.

"Oh my goodness, T-Boy's a fish!" his momma said.

"A big red fish," his daddy said.

"No time to explain," T-Boy said. "Put the nets down. The shrimp are coming."

His parents put the nets down, and the *Joie De Vivre* had the best shrimping night it would ever have. T-Boy's daddy used his radio and told all the others — the Legers, the Morvants, the Chaberts, everyone — the shrimp were running. Everyone came out and shrimped! But even with the big catch, thousands upon thousands of shrimp made it to the Gulf. The marsh stayed healthy, and T-Boy's people were happy.

Throughout the summer, T-Boy's daddy and momma sat on the dock every night and talked to him. His momma still woke him in the morning by calling out "T-Boy." But everyone else on the bayou called him Le Grand Poisson Rouge.

In late August, T-Boy began to think about his old classmates and the stories he could tell them about the world beneath the water. One night, when his momma was shelling pecans on the end of the run, he said, "Momma, I don't want to be a fish no more."

"Anymore," his momma corrected.

"Anymore. I miss my old friends, my bed, and you and daddy."

His momma tried to hide her tears, but T-Boy could see the damp streaks reflected in the moonlight.

T-Boy wished as hard as he could that he was a boy again. As his momma shook her head slowly side to side, a big tear dropped from her chin and fell right on his blunt snout. It tasted saltier than the water off Grand Isle, and before he knew it, he was a boy again — standing in the shallow water dressed just like he was the day he saved the shrimp.

"Momma, I'm me again!" he laughed.

"Yes, T-Boy. Yes."

"But Momma, the marsh heron said I could never change back."

T-Boy's momma put both her hands on his face and said, "Yes, I know, T-Boy. But there is more magic in the world than even the animals know."

To my family, for their love and support
—WTM

To the students at Yonkers Middle/High School
—GC

Author's Note

Cajuns are descendants of the French settlers who migrated to Louisiana in the 1700s, after their expulsion from Acadia (Nova Scotia, Canada). Once established in Louisiana, these Acadian settlers developed their own French-based language, music, and food. After a time, they were called Cajuns. Their characteristic hearty enjoyment of life remains a vital part of Louisiana culture even today.

Text copyright © 2002 by Wayne T. McGaw
Illustrations copyright © 2002 by George Crespo

Carolrhoda Books, Inc.
A division of Lerner Publishing Group
241 First Avenue North
Minneapolis, MN 55401 U.S.A.

Website address: www.lernerbooks.com

Library of Congress Cataloging-in-Publication Data

McGaw, Wayne T.
    T-boy of the bayou / by Wayne T. McGaw ; pictures by George Crespo.
        p.   cm.
    Summary: A heron overhears a boy's wish that he could help his father, a shrimper whose nets have been empty lately, and shows him what needs to be done to make things right.
    ISBN: 0—87614—648—5 (lib. bdg. : alk. paper)
    [1. Shrimp fisheries—Fiction. 2. Bayous—Fiction. 3. Herons—Fiction. 4. Shrimps—Fiction. 5. Magic—Fiction.] I. Crespo, George, ill. II. Title.
PZ7.M16746 Tb 2002
[Fic]—dc21   2001006942

Manufactured in the United States of America
1 2 3 4 5 6 — JR — 07 06 05 04 03 02